AN Otis Christmas

AN Otis

LOREN LONG

SCHOLASTIC INC.

It was wintertime on the farm where the friendly little tractor named Otis lived. Snow covered the hills, church bells rang through the cold wintry valley, and Christmas was almost here.

Christmas was a festive time on the farm. The farmer strung lights, hung wreaths, and trimmed the annual Christmas tree. Otis loved Christmas, but this one was even more special. One of the horses was expecting a baby foal!

Otis could hardly wait to welcome it into their farm family. He would teach the new arrival about life on the farm, and he was excited to have a new friend to play with, *putt puff puttedy chuff.*

On Christmas Eve, the farmer came to the barn and fed the animals their traditional Christmas meal of hot bran mash with chopped apples and brown sugar. Otis delighted in watching them dig in around the trough. He knew how much they loved the special treat.

While the animals were eating, the farmer opened his toolbox and brought out a package wrapped with a bow. He opened the package, pulled out a shiny horn, and said,

"Merry Christmas, Otis!" He bolted the horn onto him, saying, "A special tractor needs a special horn."

The farmer wished them all a Merry Christmas, and as he headed back to the farmhouse, he said, "Sleep tight, all, a big snow is heading our way!"

Otis was so happy, he didn't know what to do. He had never, ever received a Christmas gift before. And he had always wanted a horn like the truck had. As Otis settled into his stall for a good night's sleep, the snow started falling and he thought this was sure to be the best Christmas ever.

Putt puff puttedy zzzZZZZ.

But suddenly, Otis woke to the sound of troubled voices . . .

It was the farmer, in the horse's stall.

The horse was pacing back and forth, breathing heavily, and swinging her head up and down.

Something was wrong.

She stopped, pawed at the ground, dropped to the floor, rolled over onto her back and then to her side.

Something was *very* wrong.

Then Otis heard the farmer say something that sent chills through his frame: "We need Doc Baker out here tonight or we'll lose 'em both!"

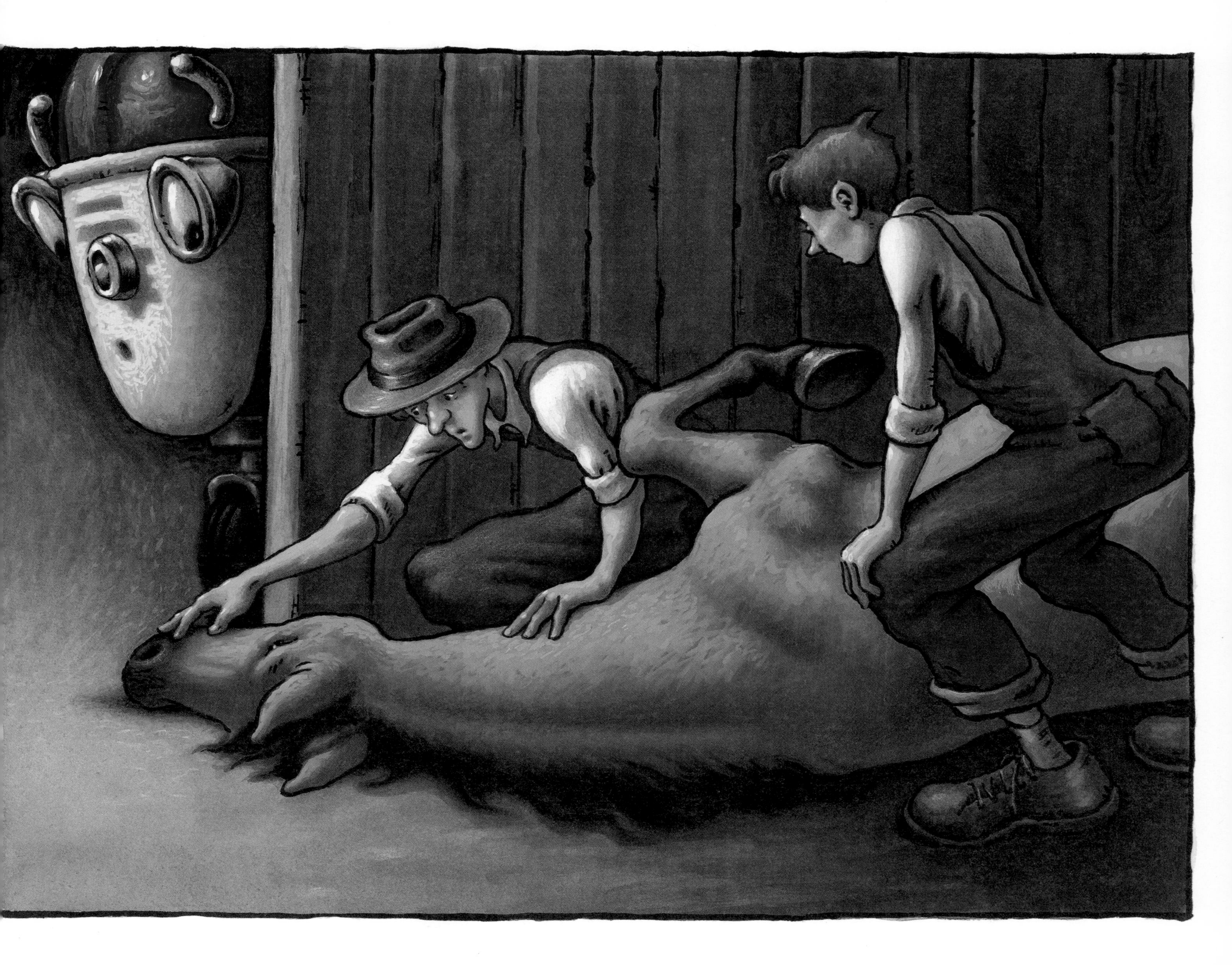

The farmer sent one of his helpers to get Doc Baker. As the barn door opened, they saw nothing but white. They were amazed at how much snow had fallen! The truck lunged forward, fishtailed this way and that, and promptly slid down the hill, plunging into a snowdrift. Otis watched as the farmhand spun the tires deeper and deeper into the snow. The truck was clearly going nowhere.

But what about Doc? And what about the sick horse?

Otis heard the farmer's words again in his head . . . "We need Doc Baker out here tonight or we'll lose 'em both!"

Otis knew where Doc lived. He had been there once delivering some supplies with the farmer. And he knew a shortcut through the woods.

With snow up to his chin, Otis headed out into the cold night to get Doc.

Otis plowed through the white woods, *putt puff puttedy chuff,* over a frozen river, across a deep meadow, and up a snowy hill to the top of a steep cliff.

And that's when Otis realized he was lost.

He had climbed the wrong hill! Everything looked different covered in snow.

There was no time to turn back.

Otis aimed his headlights over the cliff, saw where he needed to be, and bravely headed down a dangerous path.

The way down was slippery and treacherous. It took all of Otis's courage to keep going. Yet before he knew it, he had reached the bottom and could see the edge of the hollow where Doc Baker lived.

All was quiet that Christmas Eve as Otis plowed up to Doc's house. He flashed his headlights and gunned his engine, but no matter how hard he tried, no one in the house stirred.

How could Otis wake up Doc?

Of course! His shiny new Christmas horn!

As loud as Otis could muster, he blared his horn . . . *beep beep, honk honk, putt puff, beep beep honk!* A light came on and Doc Baker threw open the window. Otis reared up, *chuff*ed, and spun around in a circle.

"It looks like Otis the tractor," Doc said. "There must be trouble on the farm!"

In the twinkle of an eye, Doc dashed out the front door, jumped on Otis, and held on for dear life.

Otis sped up the hollow road and followed his tracks up and over the steep cliff, down the snowy hill, back across the deep meadow, over the frozen river, and back through the white woods. The cold wind whipped their faces as Otis and Doc Baker sped through the deep snow back onto the farm.

At the barn, the farmer and his helpers did their best to comfort the horse, who was lying still, hardly breathing. With no way of getting Doc Baker in the blizzard, there was little hope.

A hush came over the barn and the farmer prayed for a miracle.

All was quiet, until . . .

PUTT PUFF, BEEP BEEP, HONK HONK!

The farmhands threw open the door. "It's Otis, and he has Doc with him!" They ran out into the snow to help Doc Baker into the barn.

The doors closed and immediately Doc got to work. Otis stayed outside, desperately waiting to see if Doc Baker could save the horse and the little foal.

Time passed slowly as Otis *chuffed* back and forth. It had been a long night and he was exhausted. Yet he would not rest. He was too worried for his friend the horse.

Finally, Otis stopped in his tracks and looked around at the farm, all silent and covered in a blanket of peaceful snow. Daylight was near. Christmas Day would soon be upon them.

Suddenly, the barn doors opened and a warm glow poured outside. Otis heard the farmer say, "Well, would you look at that!"

When Otis *puffed* in, the animals stepped aside. There, in the middle of the barn, stood a beautiful baby foal, his spindly legs straining to keep him upright. Then Otis saw what the farmer was talking about.

The little foal had a marking the shape of a star on his forehead!

That Christmas Day, after the roads were cleared, people from all around the valley came to the barn to get a glimpse of the Christmas foal. Otis beamed with pride and realized that this certainly was the best Christmas ever. And as much as he loved his shiny new horn, Otis knew that he had more important gifts that Christmas. He had his farm family and his friends and the newborn foal, and they were the greatest gifts of all.

The End

Other books in the Otis series:

Otis

Otis and the Tornado

Otis and the Puppy

and

Otis Loves to Play

To my brothers,

Lance and Lindy.

ISBN 978-0-545-79598-2

Published by Scholastic Inc., 557 Broadway, New York, NY 10012,
by arrangement with Philomel Books, a division of Penguin Young Readers Group,
a member of Penguin Group (USA) LLC, A Penguin Random House Company.

12 11 10 9 8 7 6 5 4 3 2 1 14 15 16 17 18 19/0

Printed in the U.S.A. 08

First Scholastic printing, November 2014

Edited by Michael Green
Design by Semadar Megged
Text set in Engine
The art was created in gouache and pencil.